Hattie's
New Century

Nola L. McDonald

Edited by Robert McDonald

Cover photo furnished by Nola L. McDonald

Cover Designed by Brittany J. Jackson

Published by G Publishing LLC
P. O. Box 24374
Detroit, MI 48224

ISBN 13: 978-0-9820002-2-9
ISBN 10: 0-9820002-2-7

Library of Congress Control Number: 2008907280

Printed in the United States of America

TABLE OF CONTENTS

MY THANKS TO:

My son and editor, Robert McDonald, for his valuable advice.

Crocker House secretary, Marcia Swiderski, who found the old pictures and put them into usable form on her computer.

Erin Brown, a historical collection specialist at the Pawnee Bill Museum in Pawnee, Oklahoma.

My husband Tom for his support and encouragement.

My publisher, Julia Hunter, who brought it all together.

CHAPTER ONE

AN ILL-OMENED BEGINNING

This great new century wasn't even a week old, but in spite of living in a world-famous town and having a splendid family, my personal future looked grim.

My teacher Miss Withers, and my principal, Miss Keeler, decided that this was the week I would move ahead to sixth grade. It was a great honor. I had to admit that I had been ahead of the other fifth graders all year. I knew my time's tables through 12 times 12 and I was halfway through the *Riverside Sixth Reader.*

Miss Keeler and I walked through the upstairs hall, where the floors gave out a faint oily smell. Grant School was almost three years old now. The fifth, sixth, seventh and eighth grade rooms fronted on the large hallway. Our school library was at the back of the building and overlooked the playground.

I was nervous as I walked into Miss Holt's sixth grade class. Miss Keeler stood behind me and said, "Class, I hope you'll welcome Hattie Hoffmier to your room. She's been such an excellent student in Miss Wither's fifth grade that we've decided to promote her mid-year."

I was already fearful. My friend Elizabeth Schalm told me some stories about life in the sixth grade, and that little speech did not help my confidence a bit.

I looked at Miss Holt for reassurance. She was a handsome woman, quite stylish in her white shirtwaist with the leg-o-mutton sleeves. Even as I admired her style I wondered who ever thought of naming those puffy sleeves after a sheep's leg. She wore a long black skirt with a small bustle at the back that made it stand out with just the right lift.

"Well, here's the famous Hattie Hoffmier," she said. "Miss Smarty, come to join us from fifth grade. We'll be sure to welcome such an erudite student to our lowly classroom." The tone was pure acid.

I could hardly contain my indignation, but this wasn't the time to call attention to myself. I sat down quietly in the seat Miss Holt indicated and began to look around the room. I saw five rows of desks larger than the ones in fifth grade. Their wrought iron legs were fastened to the floor. At the front of each desk was the seat for the student in the desk ahead. I saw the familiar holes in the upper right hand corners where we could put our ink bottles.

I had been almost the shortest girl in fifth grade. In sixth grade I felt like a midget. I smiled at Miriam Rick and Shirley Goulette as we started off for lunch. They turned their backs to me.

When we left school only Elizabeth, who lived down the street, was there to walk home with me. We walked gingerly through the slushy snow down Robertson Street and turned on to an even sloppier Smith Street.

"Miss Holt doesn't like me," I said.

"Don't let her get you down, Hattie," said Elizabeth. Miss Holt is just about the meanest woman in the whole world. She has a tongue like a snake. She told John Horne that he'd surely end up a beggar when he came in late the second time in four days.

The whole class missed recess for a whole week when Earl Snay tracked mud in from the playground.

I was relieved to have at least one ally. Elizabeth's support would make it easier to face the afternoon.

My hair ribbon went flying. Luckily it missed the mud. I picked it up and retied it. My fine, almost white blond hair was a trial to me. Ribbons did not want to stay fastened.

Elizabeth had curly red hair that fell down to her shoulders. Lucky her! She hated her freckles, but I guess every redhead I know has to put up with them. My face wasn't really pretty, but I thought my green eyes and small nose wouldn't stop a trolley. Ma said, "Pretty *is* as pretty *does*." I think it's a lot easier to be good if people think you're pretty.

I plodded home worrying about Miss Holt. I was not used to a teacher's enmity. It would do no good to complain to Ma or Pa. They were proud of my promotion and expected me to do well.

My family had high expectations for the new century. Pa had a good job at Donaldson's making buggies and plows. Bill worked at a greenhouse and Clara was a waitress at the Colonial Hotel. We had a used piano in the parlor and Ma had a new-fangled washer with a wringer that turned with a crank. Best of all, our house had an indoor bathroom with a claw-footed cast iron bathtub and a flush toilet with a water tank high on the wall.

In this year of 1900 our small Michigan town of Mount Clemens was a famous spa. People came from all over the world to take its healing mineral baths. It had hotels, theaters, restaurants, stores and dozens of boarding houses. Just last year the electric trolley cars reached us from Detroit. We can travel clear to New Baltimore now. Last year my brother John earned a free ticket to The Stetson's spectacular *Uncle Tom's Cabin.* He got it for hanging on to the leashes of three bloodhounds during the street parade.

It always gratified me to climb the two steps to the front porch on our 1897 Homestead house. The gingerbread latticework around the porch roof was so elegant. The carpenter got the plans for our place from a book. The two-story house was T-shaped with a summer kitchen added on to the back. We had gaslights on the walls but still used kerosene lamps for close work. "Never blow out a gas light," Ma warned us.

"Always use the valve. You don't want the house to blow up, do you?"

But today I wasn't admiring the house. I was thinking of the second dilemma that had me troubled.

CHAPTER TWO

PROBLEMS AT HOME

Soon after Christmas Pa got all of us together in the kitchen. We all sat around the pedestal table with the two extra leaves in it. There was a hole wearing through the red and white checked oilcloth that covered the grainy top. I was facing the glass-doored cupboards that held our eating utensils. Closed cupboards below contained the pots and pans.

We knew that there was something serious on Pa's mind because my seventeen-year-old brother, Bill, was there along with my fifteen-year-old sister, Clara. Bill was usually either working at

Breitmeyer's Greenhouse or off somewhere with his friends. Clara spent a lot of her time waitressing at the Colonial Hotel. My ten-year-old brother John and I sat at the table. Two-year-old Robert sat on Ma's lap. He pulled at the hairpins holding Ma's dark brown hair in a bun at the top of her head.

Pa's sandy hair fell down on his forehead. He cleared his throat just like he always did when he had something serious to say. "You know my ma isn't doing so well. She can't manage that big farm with all those vegetables to raise, not to mention the chickens and geese." Robert got down off Ma's lap and ran past the pot-bellied heating stove into our sitting room. As usual, it was my job to run after him. I returned with the little captive on my hip.

Pa continued. "Since my father died last year she's only had a hired hand to help her. My brother Joe has his own farm to run, and I can't keep going clear out to Harper all the time. Joe and I persuaded her to sell the farm. She's spry enough and heaven knows there's nothing wrong with her mind, but seventy is just too old for all that work. We talked it over with her and your Ma and I decided that since Joe and Asenath just don't have the room, she should come to Mount Clemens and live with us. Jim Horn, the hired man, is going to stay on the place until it's sold, so she'll be moving in with us next week."

"Next week!" Ma looked stunned.

"I thought we had a month or so to get ready," she said.

Pa had his *master of the house* look that he used on serious occasions.

"She's my ma, Emma. I knew you'd want her here just as soon as possible."

Ma didn't say anything else, but I had heard her talking to Clara about how opinionated and set in her ways Grandma Hoffmier was.

"Where will she sleep?" asked Clara.

Pa was still being king of the castle. "Well, you will be moving upstairs with Hattie, and Grandma will have your room behind the kitchen."

Clara was outraged. "You mean I have to share that tiny upstairs room with Hattie?"

"Clara" said Ma, "We can't expect Grandma to climb those stairs all the time. She'll be nice and warm next to the kitchen."

"Why can't she stay somewhere else?" asked Clara.

"Do you want to send her out to the poor farm?" Pa was angry. Having to go to the poor farm was the most shameful thing a family could face.

"Couldn't she rent a room some place?" asked Clara. "There are boarding houses all over town!"

"And who'd pay for that? You, Clara?" Now Ma was angry too.

Clara closed her mouth, but she clomped off, slamming things around as she got ready to move her belongings from the small room behind the kitchen to the even smaller room upstairs that she was going to share with me. My heart sank. Clara was a slob. She was always losing her little lace caps and starchy aprons that she had to wear for waitressing at the Colonial Hotel. Her room was a disaster.

Bill and John didn't say a word. They were used to sharing a room. I could tell that they thought the whole thing between Clara and me was hilarious. John stuck out his tongue. He was a year younger than I, but he thought being a boy made him superior. Ma and Pa let him do things they wouldn't even consider for me.

We climbed the stairs to where three of our bedrooms faced a front hallway. Ma and Pa slept in the front room. They had a big walk-in closet for storage. Robert's crib was in the middle room. It had a small pot-bellied stove that Pa lit on the coldest nights. My room, now Clara's and mine, was at the end of the hall. It had two doors. One went down a small hallway to the boys' bedroom. That hall also passed by our modern bathroom. We didn't have ewers and basins on our dresser like in the old house. There was a real sink with running water. No more bathing in the kitchen and carrying buckets of hot water.

"Get used to life being unfair!" Clara told me as we rearranged our room that night. "Pa wouldn't let me go to high school. He said it was a waste of money to educate a girl who would just up and get married."

Sometimes I hated being a girl.

Robert didn't have to worry. He could toddle around in his little lacey dresses carrying my old rag doll. His crib was secure!

So except for Robert, we worked hard to get ready for Grandma Hoffmier.

New century or not – what a muddle!

CHAPTER THREE

SCHOOL AGAIN

The class chanted:

"Maine, Augusta on the Kennebec.
New Hampshire, Concord on the Merrimac.
Vermont, Montpelier on the Onion River.
Massachusetts, Boston on the Boston Harbor."
And on and on through all 45 states.

I daydreamed. I already knew all the states and capitals. My Webster's Blue Book Speller was on my desk. The sixth grade words were no challenge.

Friday afternoon's spelling bees gave me a chance to shine.

Grant School

Yesterday, Dan Poling had asked me to help him with his words for the week. He did well in everything but spelling. "I just can't get the hang of it!" he admitted.

"He's sweet on you," said Elizabeth. She was always trying to put all of us in pairs. Dan has a pleasing voice, and is friendly to both Elizabeth and me, but I'm not *sweet* on anyone.

"Here's how we learned hard words in fifth grade," I told him. We made up a silly sentence for a word that was bothering us. For 'arithmetic' we said *A rat in the house may eat the ice cream.* The first letter in each word helped us remember. For "geography" we used *George Elliot's old grand-mother rode a pig home yesterday.*

"That's a great idea, Hattie. I'll have to try it."

Dan was always getting himself into a fix with words.

"Last week he mispronounced fatigue, calling it "fat-I-gue" as if it rhymed with "glue." Miss Holt made him come to the front of the class and say it correctly thirty times.

"Now," she said, "You must be too *fat-I-gued* to go out to recess, so you can stay in and write the word fifty times on the blackboard."

That same morning Ben Stone had to sit in the corner for an hour with a dunce cap on his head because he was late coming in from recess.

"I'd rather take a wallop than sit on that stool with a stupid cone hat on my head," he told every-one.

Elizabeth and I felt sorry for Ben, and all three of us longed to see the caustic Miss Holt humbled.

Miss Holt *was* mean to everyone. But I stayed out of her way and did my work. Her one good quality was that she read to us the last half-hour of every day. Her voice was clear and she read with such feeling I was carried into the story.

She was well into *Little Women* by Louisa May Alcott when I joined the class. Clara had given the book to me last Christmas, and even though I knew the story well, I was enthralled against my will. Her rich voice had a catch in it as she read, "A dreadful fear passed coldly over Jo as she thought 'Beth is dead and Meg is afraid to tell me' The fever flush and the look of pain were gone, and the beloved little face looked so pale and peaceful in utter repose that Jo felt no desire to weep or lament. Leaning low over this dearest of her sisters, she kissed the damp forehead with her heart on her lips, and softly whispered, 'Good-by, my Beth, Good-by.'"

I knew that Beth was not dead at that point, but it was all I could do to keep from sobbing.

CHAPTER FOUR

THE BAD LUCK DAY

Anyone whose birthday is on April Fool's Day cannot expect things to go smoothly. Pa thought Ma was trying to trick him twelve years ago and almost didn't go for the midwife. But April Fool's Day was not the cause of my misfortune.

Miss Holt had a frown on her face all morning. "How can you be so stupid?" she said when some of the boys didn't understand long division.

"This time listen to me. I'll try to simplify it so that even the most dull-witted can grasp the concept." She had that contemptuous tone again.

It was a beautiful day, the first nice day of spring.

"Come on, Hattie," Elizabeth begged. You haven't been out to recess all week. You can't stay in on your birthday!"

I had promised to organize the sixth grade bookcase full of fiction and put the books in alphabetical order by author, like a "real" library. I'd been working at recess time all week, but there were still piles of books all over the back of our room.

"You can finish next week," coaxed Elizabeth. "A day like today is a birthday gift to you."

That was true. April first was bright and balmy. The books could wait.

Elizabeth and I didn't head for the Red Rover game, where each team dared someone to cross over and break through lines of players with arms held together. One side would shout together, "Red Rover, Red Rover, Send Hattie right over." If I broke through, I got to take a prisoner back to my side and if I didn't I was caught and had to join the enemy. Being short and lightweight, I was always captured.

"Not today," I decided.

It would have been a good day for jumping rope, but mine was at home. So we sat on the back steps of Grant School reading Elizabeth's autograph book. Chloe had written-

> "When you are sitting all alone
> Reflecting on the past
> Remember that you have a friend
> That will forever last."

"Here's my favorite," said Elizabeth.

> "The large are not the sweetest flowers
> The long are not the happiest hours.
> Much talk does not a friendship tell.
> Few words are best. I wish you well."

"That's too flowery," I said. "I like them short and snappy. Here's a good one."

> "If you see a monkey up a tree
> Pull its tail and think of me."

"Or what about this one?"

> "When you are old and washing dishes
> Remember me and my good wishes."

"Autographs are supposed to be sentimental," said Elizabeth. "Here's a perfect one. It's short, but not silly like the ones you chose."

> "In the golden chain of friendship,
> Regard me as a link."

All of the messages were written in flowing script with pen and ink. All of our friends prided themselves on being able to write letters that moved gracefully across the page. I tried hard to imitate the lovely letters, but alas, I did not excel in handwriting.

The bell rang. Miss Holt came to the door and frowned at us. The familiar ridges between her eyes warned of trouble ahead. When the class trooped back into the room and everyone was seated, she walked over to the shelves where several dozen books were scattered on the floor.

"Well, Miss Hattie Hoffmier," Her arms were crossed and her voice dripped sarcasm. "You may be a smart, young lady, but you'll never amount to anything. You never finish what you start."

"But, Miss Holt," I tried to explain.

"Not another word." She glared at me. "I'll know better than to depend on you again."

I willed myself not to let the tears spill down my cheeks.

It was time to get serious about the Miss Holt plan. Elizabeth, Dan, Ben and I agreed to meet at Ben's house on Robertson Street after school to discuss ideas for revenge. We invited my brother John. He's only in fourth grade, but he has a genius for sly tricks.

Ben's ma had chores for him to do, so we put off our meeting until next week.

CHAPTER FIVE

GRANDMA HOFFMIER

Grandma Hoffmier moved in the third week in January with the help of Pa, Uncle Joe and her hired man. Uncle Joe's wagon carried her brass bedstead, a dresser with a mirror, her favorite rocking chair, and her big black cast iron stove. She sat on the wagon seat with a large gray tabby cat on her lap.

"Be careful with that kitchen range," Grandma ordered. "Grandpa got it for me just two years ago."

The men struggled to get the big iron heater through the back door into our summer kitchen. It was huge even though the water heater on the side had been removed.

With the addition of Grandma's things, some of our own furniture got moved upstairs to our bedrooms.

"I told you we'd be too crowded!" complained Clara as we strove to put our belongings in some order. But she knew better than to say anything in Grandma's presence.

Life with Grandma Hoffmier was a challenge. She was always telling us what to do. She brought this book from the farm with her called *The Household Guide or Domestic Encyclopedia, Home Remedies for Man or Beast*. She kept it handy on her dresser. It had advice about everything in the world. It told how to shoe a balky horse. We didn't have a horse. How to cure warts on your face, how to nurse a sick pig. It gave directions on how to make cookies or stews. But most of all, it gave directions on how we should act. She was always spouting rules from it for us to follow.

"Clara," she admonished, after a consultation of the book, "You should know it's vulgar to lift your skirt with both hands when you cross the street."

"Well, vulgar or not," said Clara. "I don't intend to get my skirts dirty on this muddy road."

"Clara," shouted Ma. "You will not sass your grandmother!"

When Pa had trouble sleeping one night, she got out the book. "William," she said, "It says here that you should lie with your head to the north. There's something in the electrical effects of the earth that relaxes you in that position."

Pa thought he shouldn't have eaten so much sauerkraut and wieners, but he knew from experience that it didn't do any good to argue with his mother.

John got a new etiquette rule when he said, "ugh" and spit a worm from his apple. "When a well-mannered boy finds a worm or insect in his food, he should say nothing," said Grandma. The sour look on his face gave away his opinion about that.

"Emma," Grandma said to Ma, "Don't you let those children fool with those gas lights. If they forget and blow one of them out without turning the valve, the whole house may blow up." Ma assured her that we all had been warned of the danger.

The following week the whole family got into a dreadful argument. Clara had just come home from work and was about to eat a doughnut. She was so proud of her job in the fancy dining room of the Colonial. Grecian columns held up the tall ceiling, and each table was graced with a large white cloth.

Sometimes we thought she was a little too impressed by the rich atmosphere.

The Colonial Hotel

"Michigan is such a backward state," she said. "Women can vote in Wyoming, Colorado, Utah and Idaho. Lots of the people who eat in the Colonial dining room say all women should be allowed to vote. Ma, don't you think there should be suffrage for us?"

Grandma was scandalized. "I've never heard of anything so outlandish. William, do you think you should allow that girl to go on working in a place where those snooty people put such ideas into her head?"

"I'll promise you this." replied Pa, "If women are ever allowed to vote, Emma will go along with me and vote the way I do."

Then Ma got her back up. "I may be a woman," she said. "But this woman knows there is such a thing as a secret ballot. If and when I get the vote, I'll vote as I please."

Pa escaped to go to his weekly meeting as a volunteer at the fire station, and Grandma went to her room. Clara stomped upstairs and Ma sighed. I agreed with Clara, but I didn't say anything.

When I was downcast over my problems at school, Grandma said, "Hattie, don't go around with that hangdog look. You should cultivate a happy temper. Banish the blues. A cheerful spirit begets cheer and hope." That sounded straight from the book.

Grandma thought I read too much. She found several of my hiding places where I disappear with a good book. She always managed to find something else for me to do. "Hattie, you'll ruin your eyes," she said.

Well, at least I'm not stuck in just one stupid book forever," I thought.

My grandmother and her tiresome book were still living in the nineteenth century.

CHAPTER SIX

THE MEETING

We told Ben's mother we were meeting to practice for a school play. She let us use her kitchen table and gave us milk and cookies. When she left to do some chores we got down to business.

"Squirt ink on one of her white blouses," said John.

"No," I said. "It ought to be something that looks like an accident."

"Grease the floor, or put wax on a spot near her desk. Maybe she'll fall and break a leg," said Dan.

"Put a frog or a snake in her desk," suggested Elizabeth. Her freckles were more noticeable as she considered a solution.

"No," said Ben. "Someone put a snake in her drawer in September. She just lifted it out and gave it to me to take outside. You should have heard all the girls scream."

"Did you know that no matter how early in the day a snake is killed its tail won't die until dark?" asked John.

"Yes, "said Dan. "Have you ever heard of a hoop snake? My pa knew a man who once saw one. It took its tail in its mouth and rolled away like a bicycle tire. He told him there was a stinger in its tail, and if it stung you, you'd swell up and die."

"Let's get back to the subject," said Elizabeth.

"Get the whole class to help," suggested Ben. We could all stand up together and shout, 'Miss Holt is a witch!'"

"Let's not involve any more students," I objected. "Miriam Rick and Shirley Goulette would be sure to tattle." They thought they were better than the rest of us, because their fathers were storekeepers. They brought an apple or cookie to Miss Holt every day. They sat up front in their lovely dresses. She always talked sweetly to them and gave them stars for good penmanship. If they misspelled a word they never got sent to the dunce stool.

"You know those shiny shoes she keeps under her coat?" I asked. "She changes into them when she walks to school on muddy days. We could get some stove ashes and stuff them into those shoes."

Dan had another great idea. "Let's put worms on her desk chair and hide them under the hat she keeps on that shelf in the coatroom."

"I'll get the worms," offered John, "But I won't have a chance to put them on her chair. Can you do that, Dan?"

Dan nodded.

"We can make a nasty sign to put on top of everything," Ben added.

So the plan was ready to go.

"We'll have to wait a while for the worms," I said, "The ground is still too hard."

"All we need now is a good soaking rain." said Elizabeth.

CHAPTER SEVEN

THE VARIETY SHOW

"Hattie," yelled Clara. "Ma, look what I've got." She held a hand behind her back and danced around the kitchen.

"What is it?" asked Ma.

"Two fifty-cent tickets to tomorrow night's variety show at the Nelson Opera House," said Clara. "One of the actors is staying at the Colonial, and he gave them to Stella and me."

"Oh, Clara," I said. "You are so lucky!"

"Well, Hattie, maybe you're lucky, too. Stella can't go tomorrow night. She has an evening shift as a rubber in the bathhouse. She'll be giving massages to her rich clients. She can't afford to lose the tips. Would you like to go with me?"

"Oh, Ma, may I?" I begged.

"Hattie, it's a school night."

"Maaa!" Clara and I both moaned.

"Oh, all right." Ma gave in. "If Pa agrees."

We both danced around the kitchen. We knew Pa wouldn't object.

The next day even Miss Holt's sour face couldn't faze me, but the day was endless.

At home I had to search the chicken coop for eggs and help Ma with supper. Clara hurried home from work, but it still took us an hour and a half to get ready to go. Clara used the curling iron on my fly-away hair. She knew how to heat it to just the right temperature on the old coal stove in the summer kitchen. I felt quite elegant with curly bangs. Clara's long hair was a darker blond than mine. She pinned two small pillow-like puffs called "rats" to the top of her head and combed her hair back over them into a pompadour.

My good dress was a blue muslin with a white lace collar and puffed sleeves. The skirt was almost ankle-length.

Clara had to have Ma help her get laced into her corset.

"Emma," said Grandma. "It can't be healthy for a body to be laced so tightly." For once there didn't seem to be anything in her book that fit the occasion.

Clara's lacy sleeves were short and she had long white gloves. Blue satin ribbons came over her shoulders and met the one that circled her tiny waist. The neckline was low and square.

Pa came home just in time to see us off. "Emma," he said. "My little girls are little no more. We've got two elegant young ladies here tonight." Clara and I just beamed.

For a change it wasn't muddy and we were able to walk up Kibbee Street to the trolley car on Gratiot without getting a mark on our high-button shoes. The spring evening was warm, but we didn't walk the mile into town.

"We want to get there looking as good as when we started out," said Clara as we paid our nickels and rode the trolley to Cass Avenue. We walked the last block down Cass to the Nelson Opera Theater.

It was already crowded. Clara had been given fifty-cent tickets, so we had good seats on the main floor.

"Oh, Clara," I sighed. "The theater is magnificent!"

Clara had been there before, but it was all new to me. The stage curtains were a deep purple velvet. The lights were electric instead of gas like we had at home. There were gold columns around the sides of the auditorium. The ceiling had plaster relief work and murals.

"Hattie, look at the balcony," said Clara.

The balustrade was open work and the second floor was as full of people as the main floor.

The curtains opened, and the show was all that I dreamed it could be. The first act was a juggler. I was mesmerized as he kept balls and nine pins and then six plates in the air at one time.

Rosie O'Grady, the singer, was next. She sang "My Wild Irish Rose" and "When Irish Eyes Are Smiling."

A comedy team, Hatcher and Hart came on stage. Hatcher said, "I'll never eat any more of your mother's pies."

Hart came back with, "Why, my mother was baking pies before you were born."

"I know she was," said Hatcher. "I just ate one of them."

I fell off my seat I was laughing so hard. The next joke was even funnier.

"And so you were born on Thanksgiving Day" said Hatcher.

"Yes sir," answered Hart.

"Then your parents have something to be thankful for, haven't they?"

"Yes, sir; they say they're thankful I ain't twins." I fell off my seat again.

"Hattie, if I have to pick you up off the floor one more time, I'm taking you home," scolded Clara.

"I can't help it, Clara. They're so funny."

Then came some acrobats, the Patchin Brothers. There were three of them. They did hand stands and flip-flops and pyramids and were all over that stage so fast, I could hardly keep track of them.

But the last act was the best. An actor and elocutionist named DeWolf Hopper recited a poem called "Casey at the Bat" by Ernest Thayer.

"I've been reciting this poem regularly since 1888 when I introduced it at Wallack's Theater in New York," said Mr. Hopper.

I had never heard it before. It was about a baseball game in Mudville. The home team was losing, but the spectators knew they would have a chance if only their star, Casey, could get up to bat. That didn't look likely. Casey made it up to the plate, but he was so arrogant he purposely let the first two pitches go by. It's true that pride goes before a fall. When it got to the part where Casey took that last swing, the audience was on the edge of their seats.

Mr. Hopper said, "There was no joy in Mudville. Mighty Casey has struck out."

We all groaned.

Everyone stood up and clapped for Mr. Hopper. "That," said Clara, "is called a 'standing ovation' and only happens when an act is especially good."

But the night wasn't over. After the performance the manager came on stage. "Ladies and Gentlemen," he said. "In two weeks we will be sponsoring an Elocution Contest for young people ages eleven to fourteen. First prize will be five dollars. Second prize will be four free tickets to George Stetson's spectacular 'Uncle Tom's Cabin' this June. And third prize will be a silver dollar and a framed certificate."

"Prospective contestants can see me next week at the theater office," he added.

"Hattie, you should enter that contest," said Clara.

"Oh, Clara, I'd be too scared," I said. But I couldn't get the idea out of my head.

CHAPTER EIGHT

ELOCUTION LESSONS

"I wish you could have gone with us, Elizabeth. It was a magic night!" I told her all about the exciting acts we saw at the Nelson Theater, and of course about the contest.

"Clara is right," she said. "You read aloud so beautifully."

"Well, when I was in fifth grade Mrs. Withers would have me read to the class. We had to memorize pieces of poetry or give speeches every Friday afternoon." Reciting pieces was not new to me. Maybe I could do it.

On Monday Elizabeth and I went uptown and knocked at the side door of the Nelson Opera House.

"You're pretty little," said the manager. "Are you sure you want to compete?"

I wasn't sure at all, but "Yes Sir," I assured him.

"She's older than she looks," said Elizabeth.

Soon I was registered officially. It was too late to back out.

"I know just what I'm going to do," I told her on the way home. "Did you ever hear the poem, *Somebody's Mother?*

"No," she said.

"It was published in the *Mount Clemens Monitor.* I cut it out. It's tucked away in my box of treasures. Oh, it's so sad," I told her. "It's about an old lady who's trying to cross a snowy street and is scared of all the horses and wagons. I already know the beginning."

The woman was old
And ragged and gray.
And bent with the chill
Of the winter's day.
The street was wet
With the recent snow,
And the woman's feet
Were aged and slow.

Nobody stopped to help her until a group of boys came by on their way home from school. One boy stayed behind to see her across the street. He told his friends·

'She's somebody's mother
Boys, you know'
For all she's aged
And bent and slow.'

It ends —

'And somebody's mother
Bowed low her head
In her home that night
And the prayer she said,
Was "God be kind to that
noble boy,
Who is somebody's son
And pride and joy.'"

"Oh," said Elizabeth. "That's heart·rending. Is it very long?"

"It's long, but I already know part of it."

We talked to Mrs. Keeler the next day to see if I could practice in our library after school. "Of course," she said. "Good luck, Hattie. I'll have to get a ticket to see the contest."

All this was exciting to me, but what happened next was unbelievable.

Elizabeth was listening to me in the library when who should appear but Miss Holt. I stopped in mid-sentence. "What's she doing here," I whispered to Elizabeth.

"Go on, Hattie," said Miss Holt. "Mrs. Keeler asked me to help you out. I've had some experience with elocution. Let me hear your piece."

"Yes, Miss Holt." I began again, trying to keep the shake out of my voice.

Miss Holt just listened as I went through the whole thing. "Hattie," she said, "Your expression is excellent, but you have to project your voice. Performing in a theater is a lot different from reciting in a classroom."

She sounded firm but her voice lacked the usual caustic tone.

"Open your mouth sufficiently. You need to be heard at the back of the auditorium. Articulate – each word or syllable should come out in a full round tone.

"Elizabeth, I want you to go out in the hall and tell me if you can hear her," she ordered.

Elizabeth did as she was told and I tried again and again.

Finally, Miss Holt said, "That's enough for now, Hattie. Elizabeth, you can go along home. Hattie, if you can walk home with me, I have some books that might help you."

"Elizabeth, will you let Ma know where I am?" I was glad that Miss Holt couldn't tell what I was thinking. I should have been grateful for the help, but I could hardly bear the thought that I'd be under her thumb even after school.

We walked up Robertson Street to Gratiot. Across from the Colonial hotel was a large boarding house. Miss Holt opened the front door and I followed her up the front stairs. She went into a room where an obscenely fat old woman sat in a large rocking chair.

"Ruth" said a querulous voice. "You are late. I need help to get ready for dinner."

"Yes, mother," said Miss Holt. "I've been helping one of my students. We still have plenty of time." She went over to a bookcase with glass doors and took out a book. It was called *Brooks Manual of Elocution and Reading.*

"Pay particular attention to the practice exercises for lips and tongue, and I'll see you again tomorrow after school."

"Ruth" said her mother. "Does that mean you'll be late again tomorrow?"

"Possibly, Mother," Miss Holt said wearily.

I thanked her and carried that book home carefully. "Woe is me," I thought. "If I should damage it, my life wouldn't be worth living." At home I got down to work. If Miss Holt or her book could help me win the contest I'd just have to put up with her.

The manual told about the Delsarte method of speaking. The idea was that a person's body and mind should act together when public speaking. It had pictures of famous speakers and was illustrated with photos that showed how a person should stand and gesture to show certain emotions like defiance, remorse, exaltation or horror. I had no idea that such things could be taught.

It gave exercises to improve diction. That's where she told me to start.

"Round the rough and rugged rocks the ragged rascal ran," I chanted.

"Emma," called Grandma. "Your youngest daughter is going crazy."

"Peter Prangle, the prickly pear picker picked three pecks of prickly, prangy pears, "I continued practicing the tongue twisters that were supposed to improve my diction.

Ma gave me a few days' grace away from my chores. "Ma, it's not fair!" said John.

Amazingly, Grandma championed me. She listened to me from the kitchen as I recited from the second floor landing.

John kept on complaining. "I can't listen to this one more time. I'm about ready to kill that poor old woman, ragged and gray as she may be."

The whole family teased me, but I knew they'd all be there for the competition.

Miss Holt was there in the library after school each day. "Go home, you're nothing but a distraction," she told Elizabeth the second evening.

The day before the contest I returned her precious book. I wasn't sure how I would do, but I knew that my expression was good and that even someone in the last row of the theater would be able to hear me.

Miss Holt didn't give me any praise. She said, "Well, Hattie, I've done all I can. It's up to you now."

What was I going to do about Miss Holt? She had been helping me all week. The next warm rain would bring out the earthworms for our planned revenge. Maybe our group needed to rethink things in another meeting.

An Elocutionist

CHAPTER NINE

THE ELOCUTION CONTEST

O ur whole family was at the theater. Uncle Joe, Aunt Asenath and almost all the cousins were there. Ma, Pa, Bill, Clara and John had paid for quarter seats. Grandma was taking care of Robert. I sat up on the stage with nine other contestants.

We drew numbers for our turns. I was number five. I don't think I could have managed to say a word if I had been first. I could see Elizabeth seated up front with my family. I couldn't see whether Miss Keeler, Mrs. Withers, and Miss Holt had come. The new electric stage lights shone in my eyes and things were hazy after the first few rows.

The first contestant was a boy named John Schalm. He was loud enough, but his words came out all mushy. "Articulate!" I wanted to tell him.

Next was a girl from Macomb School. She got to the front of the stage and froze. She stood there for what seemed an eternity, took a handkerchief from her pocket and ran tearfully off the stage.

Number three, a tall boy named Richard McKee, was a force to reckon with. He did a poem called "Which Shall It Be?" about an impoverished father and mother trying to choose which of their children to give away to a rich uncle. They went from bed to bed looking at each sleeping child and of course decided that they couldn't spare even one of their brood. I could hear every word plainly and he spoke with lots of feeling. The audience clapped a lot.

Boy Number Four made it through Lincoln's *Gettysburg Address* in record time.

Then it was my turn. I took a deep breath and walked to the front of the stage. "*Somebody's Mother*, by Mary Dow Brine," I started. My voice was clear. I didn't make any mistakes. At the end there was a catch in my voice as I ended, "God take care of that wonderful boy, Who's somebody's son and pride and joy." I bowed and went back to my seat. I could hear my family and schoolmates and the rest of the audience clapping.

I did it! I came through without disgracing myself.

I was too wound up to hear much of the next four performances. But when Glenn Rieck, number ten, reached the front of the stage I began to listen again. He seemed a little older than the rest of us.

Glenn's voice was loud and clear. "Good evening," he said. I would like to recite for you *"The Mountain Whippoorwill"* by Steven Vincent Benet. *"* His poem told the story of a Georgia Mountain boy who entered a fiddling contest and ended up beating the best fiddlers in the state. Each syllable was perfect. He articulated, all right! His voice sounded like a fiddle at times. When he finished, women were getting out their handkerchiefs. The clapping was tremendous.

The Judges were seated at different places in the audience. Now they gathered together in front of the stage. There were three men and two women. It didn't take them long to decide the winners, but it seemed forever to me. Two of the men had gray hair and whiskers. One was younger and very tall. The women both had their hair in pompadours like Clara wore when she dressed up. They sat together talking and I could see them nod to each other and motion to the theater manager.

It was he who made the announcement. "Third Place and a silver dollar goes to Hattie Hoffmier for *Somebody's Mother.*" I stood up and went to the front of the stage again. "Second place is won by Richard McKee for his rendition of *Who Shall It Be.* He'll receive four free tickets to this theater's June production of *Uncle Tom's Cabin.* And first place," (This was no surprise to anybody.) "Goes to Glenn Rieck for his *Mountain Whippoorwill.*"

The clapping filled the theater again.

It was gratifying to win a prize. I knew the judges were fair. The rows were starting to empty when I came off the stage. Ma and Pa were standing by the stage steps to give me hugs. Bill and Clara said, "We're so proud of you!" John clapped me on the shoulder. Dan Poling was right behind him. Elizabeth gave me a hug. Even Miss Keeler and Mrs. Withers came up to congratulate me. I didn't see Miss Holt.

The next day at school, I waited anxiously for Miss Holt's words. We did our sums and worked on our essays and followed our usual schedule. Miss Holt said little, but her frowns indicated a storm brewing. It wasn't until the end of the day, when everyone was seated awaiting dismissal that she said, "Well, class, our smart little shining star was outshone. She came in a poor third in the elocution contest. I'm embarrassed to have spent so much time coaching a loser."

Most of my classmates just gasped. Miriam Rick and Shirley Goulette gave me sly grins. Elizabeth stared in disbelief. This time I couldn't hold back the tears. I ran sobbing to the coatroom and prayed for a soaking rain to bring out the spring worms.

CHAPTER TEN

SWEET REVENGE

That evening our secret group met again. "I'll get the worms for her desk chair," said Dan.

Helpful John said, "There's an ash pile behind our house. I'll get a little box of them to carry to school. Hattie can dump them in those shiny black boots of hers." Elizabeth enlisted her big sister to paint a sign on a piece of wood saying, "MISS HOLT IS A WITCH". Ben was to see that it got in place on her desk.

Wednesday night it rained and rained.

"I've got the can of worms," said Dan, Thursday morning on the way to school

---

"Here's the sign my sister made," Elizabeth showed us cotton sack.

John had his box of ashes stashed behind a bush on the playground. All we needed was a little bit of luck and that nasty *lady* would get her just desserts.

Afternoon recess things all came together. Miss Holt had gone down to Miss Keeler's office for some reason. Elizabeth was the lookout. Dan dumped the can of squirming worms on her chair cushion and covered it with her hat from the cloakroom.

I had hidden the container of ashes from John in my desk that morning. Ben put the "witch" sign on her desk and I took the neatly blackened boots from under her coat, sat them by the wormy chair and filled them to the brim with the grimy ashes.

We merged with the other upper grade children on the playground. No one noticed our transgressions. Elizabeth and I joined our friends jumping rope. Dan sat on the steps whittling a piece of wood. John and his friend Otto had drawn a circular line in the dirt and were playing marbles. When Miss Withers came to the door and rang the bell, we all trooped inside.

We were all in our seats before Miss Holt came back into the room. "What's this?" she asked when she saw the hat on her chair. She lifted it her face turned beet red. Then she saw the sign on her desk, and looked down at the ash-filled boots. Her face crumpled. She wasn't exactly crying. It was more like she was gasping for breath. She left the room with a whirl of skirts.

A few minutes later Miss Keeler marched into the room. "Boys and girls," she said, "I am so disappointed in your despicable behavior. Miss Holt has gone home for the rest of the day. I want to see this mess cleaned up immediately. Never here at Grant School has a teacher been treated so miserably. When I find the culprits responsible, you can be sure they will be severely punished. Does anyone have anything to say?"

No one did. Our actions had gone unnoticed. The usual tattletales had nothing to tattle about. Most of the class helped in the clean up.

I should have felt triumphant, but the enormity of what we'd done began to sink in. Elizabeth, Dan and I were strangely silent on the way home. I'm scared," said Elizabeth.

"She deserved it," said Dan.

John came running up and we had to tell him everything that happened.

Dan and Ben went on down Church Street and Elizabeth went up her porch steps. John and I walked silently the rest of the way home.

I didn't go in the house. It was still raining, but I walked around to the back porch and sat there on the steps. Tears rushed to my eyes. Ma opened the back door and saw me sobbing there.

"Why, Hattie," she said. "What in the world is the matter?"

"Oh, Ma," I sobbed. "I've done something really awful!"

She sat down with me and put her arm around my shoulder. Pretty soon I was telling her the whole story. "Ma, I started this whole thing. Should I go to Miss Keeler and confess? I feel so ashamed."

"Hattie, we'll have to think this through," said Ma. "Would it make Miss Holt feel better or worse to know that you were the instigator of this mis-chief?"

I thought of all the help that Miss Holt had given me for the contest. She loaned me her pre-cious books. She stayed with me after school every night for a week. I thought of her going home to that cranky mother every night. Knowing that I was the one who planned those actions would surely make the whole thing worse.

"Worse, I guess."

"What about your fellow conspirators?" she asked, "Do you think they'll be willing to confess along with you?"

That didn't merit an answer. Maybe my wicked ideas would get my best friends in serious trouble.

"Oh, Ma," I said. "I thought getting even would make happy, but it's just caused more problems."

"That's the way in this life, Hattie. Remember what you've learned in the scriptures. 'Turn the other cheek'; 'Walk another mile.' I can't tell you what to do, but even if Miss Keeler doesn't punish you, I want to know you'll never be part of anything like this again. Can I count on you for that?"

"Ma," I said tearfully, "I never want to feel so guilty again. Hurting Miss Holt just made things worse. I promise you I'll never *plan* to hurt someone again."

"Hattie," said Ma, "I can go along with your not confessing to Miss Keeler, but I can't let you go unpunished. From now until school is over, I expect you home immediately. You can take over Clara's part of the ironing and all of the flat pieces. If you have some extra time you can work on you sewing skills for the rest of May."

Clara was very particular about her uniforms and aprons. It wouldn't be easy to please her, but I was in no position to complain.

John got home as Ma and I came back in the house. "Did you tell?" he asked.

"Just about my part in it," I answered.

Miss Holt was back in school the next day. She didn't mention what had happened. She seemed tired, and quieter than usual.

The whole class was subdued. Elizabeth, Dan, Ben and I said nothing to each other, but I knew we all were worried about being caught. The rest of the school year seemed to last forever. Somehow Miss Holt's transgressions didn't seem so important any more.

I went home to the heavy work of ironing, and more ironing, and sewing until my eyes were tired. It seemed forever until the end of May and our release from school.

Revenge wasn't so sweet after all.

CHAPTER ELEVEN

THE FOURTH OF JULY

June was a busy month. Uncle Joe brought his horse into Mount Clemens and our garden was plowed and harrowed before the end of May. All of us worked hard to get the corn, green beans, and Swiss chard in the ground. The pumpkins and squash were planted and the tomato plants put out.

By the Fourth of July school wasn't on my mind at all. Ma and Grandma and Aunt Sena had spent two days baking pies and cakes and making all sorts of other good things for a picnic.

Uncle Joe and Aunt Sena came by with their big wagon clear from Fraser.

"Come on, children," said Uncle Joe. "Help us get everything on board."

We struggled to get baskets and people in among all their things and the seven children. Luckily, Bill and Clara went with friends, or we never could have managed.

"Look what I've got," I heard John whisper to our cousin Joe.

John had hidden firecrackers in his pockets. Some came free with a new pair of pants Ma bought him and he had been saving his newspaper money for more. Ma didn't like him fooling with firecrackers. A boy got his hand blown off with one last year. But Pa helped him out on the sly. John planned to give some of them to Joe.

We headed to Crocker Field just across the Clinton River. That was where the city was to have a big fireworks display when it got dark. It was almost noon when we all got down to the park near the river and found an empty picnic table.

Over at the gazebo the mayor and councilmen gave boring speeches. They talked and talked, even longer than our minister. It was too early for any of the events for children.

"Your town stinks!" yelled Joe, Jr., Uncle Joe's eldest.

"Stinky town, stinky town," parroted the younger cousins.

The mineral water pumped for the bathhouses and hotels does have a rotten egg smell, but we Mount Clemens residents were used to it.

Ma said, "Hold your nose and just bear it. That smell gives our town its prosperity."

Our cousins stopped yelling, but behind Ma's back they kept whispering, "Stinky town, stinky town!"

Lillie, their smallest, is just seven months old. Luckily, she isn't walking yet. Robert is hard enough to handle. He's a pretty little thing with his curly hair and long dresses, but he's a handful. My cousin Louise and I spent most of the day chasing after him.

In spite of that we had a great time.

"I'm stuffed," said John. There was both hot and cold potato salad, sauerkraut, baked ham, fried chicken, fresh doughnuts, angel food and devil's food cakes, and three kinds of pie.

After dinner the little ones lay on blankets in the tree-shaded wagon and we were free to wander. There were sack races and three legged races. A band played in the gazebo. The sound and smell of firecrackers was almost constant. It was a wonderful day. I didn't think things could possibly get any better. But then···.

My cousin Will saw the poster. It was big and colorful. *Pawnee Bill's Wild West Show* was coming to town on July 26. "Look," he said, "There are going to be cowboys and Indians and a herd of live buffalo."

"Yes," said John. "It says that Pawnee Bill is the white chief of the Pawnee Indians and a famous scout and trapper."

I gazed at the big poster. "The star's a woman," I was excited. "See here. The show features Miss May Lillie, the princess of the prairie and the greatest lady horseback rifle shot in the world."

Our brother Bill came up behind us and looked over our shoulders. "Last month in the Monitor I saw an item that a Miss Lillie appeared at the Monroe Casino. It said she shot the ashes off a cigar held in the mouth of a volunteer from the audience. She also shot at a match in her partner's mouth and set it on fire. I wonder if this was the May Lillie on the poster. This sounds like a great show. Hey, we can get in for just a quarter."

My cousins and I knew we'd all be begging to go. This would be the crowning event of the summer.

John said, "I'm going to be at the railroad station when the train gets in. Maybe I can get a job watering the horses. I'd work hard for a free ticket. I walked the bloodhounds when *Uncle Tom's*

Cabin paraded through the town last summer. That was almost as exciting as the show. With all those buffalo and horses there ought to be a job for me.

"I'm going to get a job, too." I claimed rashly.

"Don't be stupid," said John. "They're not going to hire a girl."

"I can work every bit as hard as you can, John Hoffmier," I shouted.

"Maybe, but you're still a girl!" he taunted.

There it was again. The idea that girls were inferior. It wasn't fair. Girls weren't supposed to go to high school. Girls weren't supposed to get dirty! Girls were too delicate to earn a ticket to a Wild West show!

And there was born my great idea. *I wouldn't go as a girl!*

"John, would you let me borrow a pair of your knickers and a cap? If I pin up my hair, I can look like a boy." I said. "Do you think the Wild West people will think I'm too small?"

John was a year younger, but he was several inches taller than I was.

"Ma will never let you do it!" said John.

"Well, Ma doesn't need to know," I said. "John, you won't tell, will you?"

"And what will you do for me?" asked John.

"I'll empty the water pan under the ice box for the rest of July."

"And?" he said.

"I'll collect the eggs, too."

"Will you clean out the hen house for me?" he asked.

That took some thought on my part. "I will."

And I whispered in his ear, "Remember, I never told Ma about your part in the plans against Miss Holt."

That was the clincher. John gave up. "I'm in."

There were games and more to eat. The Pagoda Band played, and the fireworks rocketed over the river, but all I could think about was my wonderful plan.

CHAPTER TWELVE

JULY TWENTY-SIXTH

John and I were so excited about our schemes that July flew by for us. July 20 John ran in with the *Mount Clemens Monitor*. "Ma, Hattie, listen to this. - Pawnee Bills Combined R.R. Show, Historical Wild West, Indian Museum, Grand Hippodrome, and Congress of Noted Chiefs and Cow Boys, Vaqueros, and a limitless number of special features, exhibits here next Thursday."

Bill looked over his shoulder. "It says the show is under a management which has in the past 15 years gained a most enviable reputation for dealing honestly and liberally with the public, and of presenting many features new and startling, and many feats which delight, amaze, and amuse."

John read again, "Genuine novelties and something new at reasonable prices, in place of empty bombast and brazen extortion, are what people want now and will liberally patronize."

"Ma, doesn't that sound like something worth earning a ticket to?" John asked.

"Well, it does sound exciting," said Ma. I didn't say anything.

On July 26th John and I were up long before dawn. He wore his overalls and I had on one of his old shirts and a pair of his knickers. It felt funny to have pant cuffs tight below my knees. My flyaway hair was hidden under one of his caps.

Just as we got to the kitchen Grandma came shuffling out of her downstairs bedroom.

"Oh no," I thought. "Here goes my plan!"

"What is this?" She stood there mystified.

"I'm going to earn a ticket to the Wild West Show," said John.

"And you, Miss Hattie Hoffmier, in the strange get-up?" she asked.

"I'm going too, Grandma," I told her. "I can work for a ticket as well as any boy!"

"Well, you little devil," said Grandma. "John, you start a fire in the stove. You two can't go off without a good breakfast."

I have never been so surprised in my life. Maybe having a grandma living with us wasn't so bad after all. Grandma made us bacon and eggs and fried some leftover potatoes. We were off before anyone else was up.

I rode on the back of John's bicycle. We went down Smith Street to Church and then took Moross across to Grand Avenue. Then we headed west to the Grand Trunk Railway Station. We got there just as the sun was coming up.

The Wild West show train was already parked along a siding. The engine was clear down to Hubbard Avenue. The train stretched back from there almost to the station at Grand.

At the back of the train we saw that the men had laid bridges between the flat cars. A ramp came down from the last car. In awe we watched all sorts of amazing wagons and equipment roll down the ramp to be hitched to the waiting horses and mules that had already been unloaded. Then off they went down Cass Avenue on the way to Crocker Field.

Indians rode horses with travioses dragged behind carrying their tepees and supplies. There was a steam calliope. A chandelier wagon carried the calcium lights that would hang from poles at the evening performance. Pole and Stringer wagons carried the seats and a canvas wagon held the tents that would be put up by the sledge gang. There was a butcher wagon and a refrigerator wagon with ice. Workers rode along the sides and tops of each horse or mule-drawn vehicle. You could tell that each wagon had a special purpose and each worker knew his job.

The smell of animals was overwhelming. It was all so exciting that we almost forgot that we were there to get a job. I guess half an hour went by before John said, "Come on, Hattie. Let's go back toward the engine. We've got to find the boss."

We started back to the front of the train with John walking along side his bike. Almost to the engine we saw a pair of the performers looking over the scene. The mustached man wore a fringed buckskin jacket and a large sombrero on his head. By his side was a dark-haired little woman in silk wrapper.

John whispered, "That must be Pawnee Bill. He looks just like the man on the posters."

The man noticed us and said, "Young men, if you want a job, you'd better hustle along to Crocker Field."

The woman looked at me and smiled at him. "Gordon," she said, "I'll take this little *fellow*." I could tell that she'd seen right through me.

CHAPTER THIRTEEN

CAUGHT!

John rode off on his bike and left me there by the railroad car with the bright-eyed small woman.

The man looked at me quizzically. "May, what will you do with this young person?"

"Never mind, Gordon," she said. "Go about your business. I'll tell you later." He climbed the stairs into one for the front cars.

"Why the disguise?" she asked.

"I didn't think anyone here would hire a girl," I answered.

She smiled again, "Can you iron, young lady? If you can, I have a job for you. My little maid has a toothache and all my white blouses need done. They're clean, but I'm all thumbs when it comes to laundry."

"Yes, Ma'am," I answered. If there's one thing I knew how to do by now, it was how to iron.

"I'm Hattie Hoffmier, at your service." I was glad now that I'd had all that practice with Clara's uniforms.

"You're May Lillie," I stammered. "Was that man Pawnee Bill? You called him Gordon."

"Well, that's what the Pawnee Indians used to call him and that's his stage name. His real name is Gordon Lillie and he's my husband"

We climbed the steps into the railroad car. Inside it was like an apartment. There were curtains on the windows. A table and two chairs were on one side of the car and a small horsehair sofa rested on the other side. Kerosene lamps hung on the walls.

I followed her through a curtained door. There was a bedroom there with a big iron bedstead topped with a fluffy feather bed. At the side was a huge wardrobe for clothing and a small pot-bellied stove like we used to heat Robert's room on cold nights. The chimney went right out of a circular hole in one of the railroad car windows. In front of the bed was a cushioned rocking chair. Standing by the closet was a folding ironing board. On top of the stove there were two irons heating. They were just about like the ones I used every week. By the stove was a basket where her clothes, already dampened, were rolled up and covered with a white towel.

"My skirts and jackets are all buckskin like Gordon's," she said. "But I have all these white blouses plus the bows for my neck, not to speak of my underthings. How about if I trade you six tickets in the best seats for this basket of laundry?"

I could hardly believe my good luck. She disappeared behind a screen to get dressed. Here I was with the star of the show May Lillie, Champion Rifle Shot, and Princess of the Prairie. It was hard to put my mind to the ironing. Five minutes must have passed before I tested the first iron and started doing up her white blouses and colorful neck scarves. When my iron cooled off, I traded it for the other one on top of the little stove.

Before long May came back and plunked herself down in the rocker. She had on a white shirtwaist, a long buckskin skirt, and tall leather boots. She sat a large hat on the floor beside her.

Bravely I asked, "Did you always want to be a cowgirl?"

"Mercy no," she laughed. "I grew up in Philadelphia. My father was a doctor. I never saw a show like this until Buffalo Bill's Wild West Show came to Philly the summer I was thirteen. Gordon was working there with a group of Indians. He walked my sister and I home after the show and we started writing to each other. Three years later we were married. We went back to Oklahoma where Gordon and his family lived.

"Did you start riding in the show right away?" I asked.

She walked over to a mirrored dresser and began to brush her hair.

"No," she said. "But I did get a pony as a wedding present. Gordon taught me to ride side-saddle and how to shoot. He said I had a natural eye for a target."

She pointed to a table that contained three medals she had won for her shooting. One from 1894 was engraved to the *Champion Lady Horse-back Shot of the World.*

"We decided to start our own show," She continued. "The whole Lillie family worked on it. My mother was scandalized at first. We've been on the road every season since 1888. The whole kit and kaboodle went to Europe in 1894. That's where I got my favorite horse, George. That big chestnut follows me around like a puppy. If he's not tied up, he'll come right into my tent. He seems to sense what I want him to do. You'll see what I mean at the show."

"What do you do when you're not traveling?" I asked.

"We visit my family in Philadelphia almost every year. In Oklahoma we stay in a hotel or live in a three-room cabin on Gordon's ranch. My dream is to have a home of our own, a regular house where we can have friends visit."

"You live such an exciting life," I said in awe.

"I guess it looks that way," she sighed. "We usually travel every night, so we sleep on the train. Once in a while we might be royally entertained if we have friends in a town."

"The show goes on rain or shine," she went on. "We've performed in mud that was above the horse's hooves and once this summer a rain storm came just as the show opened and in less time than it takes to tell, the arena was a miniature lake. The audience had to wade through the water to get to their seats. One night the acrobats somersaulted around in a foot of water. Gordon wasn't sure if he was giving a Wild West show or a water carnival."

Just as I finished the last blouse, Pawnee Bill came to the door. "May, we better go now. We're going to be late to the parade."

"I'm ready, Gordon," she said. "Just let me write a note so Hattie can pick up her tickets before the show."

"So it's Hattie, is it? That's why you wanted her as a helper. I never guessed she was a girl," said Gordon Lillie.

"Miss Lillie," I asked. "Could you give me a ride up Cass Avenue? I'll tell you where to let me off. I can hardly wait to get home to tell Ma."

"Aren't you going to the parade?" asked May.

"No," I said. "I'll have to change clothes or my ma will kill me."

We rode in an open carriage pulled by two matched bays. The coachman wore a top hat. Oh, I wished someone I knew could see me, but that didn't happen. They left me off at Miller Street and my feet hardly touched the ground on the two blocks home.

CHAPTER FOURTEEN

THE REST OF THE FAMILY

By the time I got home it was too late for me to go to the parade. Clara was the only one there. Pa and Bill were at work. Grandma and Ma had taken Robert on the trolley to see the parade. We had all planned to go to the evening performance.

"You should have seen Robert," said Clara. Just this month he had graduated from his long dresses and had on the sailor suit that Ma bought from the Sears-Roebuck catalog. "He looked deceptively sweet."

I was so excited I could hardly make Clara understand what I had done.

"So, we can all go to the show and sit in the 50 cent seats," I finished up. "Clara, if John earns tickets, too, maybe we can take Dan Poling along."

"Grandma is staying home with Robert," said Clara. She says she doesn't want all that noise and excitement. That means we don't have to deal with a wiggling three-year-old."

Ma and Grandma were back from the parade by noon. Robert had a brand new hobbyhorse to ride. It had a leather head and mane, fastened to a broom stick body. He rode it all the way home, and was so tired he voluntarily took a nap.

I went through the whole story again.

"Hattie, I don't know what I'm going to do with you," said Ma. "But I'll not object to having the tickets. Pa had some money he kept aside for the show, so we'll have a grand time."

She went on, "It's a shame you missed the parade. Pawnee Bill and May Lillie led it in their carriage. One of the bandwagons had a beautiful picture of Columbus landing in America. Clara, you would have loved to see all the cowboys and Indians. Hattie, there were plenty of cowgirls, too."

Grandma interrupted, "We saw Russian Cossacks in bright blue uniforms and high hats all riding spirited horses. Some of those horses had plumes on their bridles."

I'd never seen her so excited.

"Oh, you should have seen it!" said Grandma. Her eyes sparkled. "They gave a mini show by the courthouse. There were dancers, a comedian, a vocalist and even a contortionist."

"What on earth is a contortionist?" I asked.

"He's a man who can twist himself into all kinds of strange shapes" explained Ma.

John came home about 1:30 with a ticket in his hand. "They had a water wagon pulled up by the horse tent," he said. "I spent all morning filling buckets from it to take to the horse troughs. I really earned this ticket."

Once again I got to tell my story, but John was not as impressed as Clara. He had his own exciting adventure. "There was a big accident on the way to Crocker Field and I was right there." He was jumping up and down and yelling.

"What happened?" asked Clara and I at the same time.

"Well, I hung on to the back of the Number 22 Wagon on my bike. When we got to the Crocker Bridge an electric car was coming across and ran right into it. CRASH! You should have heard the racket."

He was talking so fast we could hardly understand him. "The team broke loose and ran right over the donkey boy and his three animals."

"Was anyone hurt?" I asked.

"Only the wagon driver," said John. "He went away nursing a hurt arm. Everyone on the trolley car was yelling and screaming, but no one else was hurt."

"And Clara," he added, "there was a worker there with a Kodak Camera like you got for Christmas. He was taking pictures all over the place. A man told me that he's a carpenter with the show. I can't wait for Pa to get home. Ma, they had a kitchen tent with a twenty-one foot oven and a huge dining tent for all the workers."

"All of us need to get our chores finished," said Ma. "John, you take care of the chickens. Grandma and I will get dinner. Clara, you set the table. Hattie, you get Robert out of his crib and get him washed up for dinner."

Pa left work early and by five-thirty we were all set to go. I had Robert in his nightgown, but it would be a long time before Grandma would be able to actually tuck him in. He was galloping around the house on his new hobbyhorse.

It wasn't a dressy occasion, but Pa and Bill wore new straw boaters on their heads, and Ma's summer hat had a peacock feather around the brim. John had the same knickers he wore to school. Sadly, Clara and I had nothing new to wear.

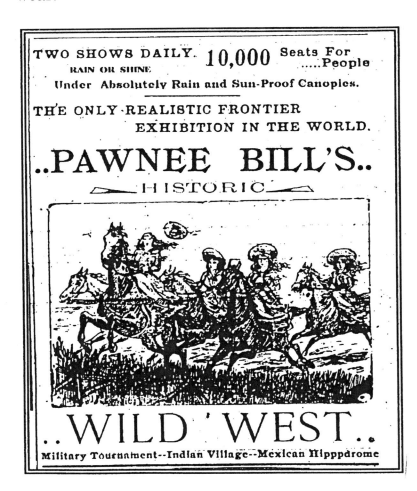

CHAPTER FIFTEEN

THE SHOW

Seven of us walked up Gratiot to Cass Avenue. John had sold his earned ticket to Dan's older brother and given Dan the quarter he got for it. Now Dan had the fifty cents for another of the more expensive seats.

We got there a little after six o'clock. The main show didn't start until 7:30. I took my note to the ticket man and got my six precious tickets.

Pa said to John and I, "Here's fifty cents for each of you. Don't spend it all in one place." Clara and Bill had their own money to use for extras.

Clara and I went for some spun sugar candy. Ma got a candy apple. Pa, Bill and the two boys headed for the side shows. We could hear a band playing from inside the side show tent.

Outside the side shows tent a barker yelled, "See the snake charmer! Marvel at the sword swallower. M'selle Van Buskirk will read your mind! Step right up. One quarter lets you in."

"Watch the half-man, half-monkey. See demonstrations of cowboy whittling and the ancient art of glass blowing. One quarter, Ladies and Gentlemen!" he went on.

Ma, Clara and I wandered around outside the arena eating our spun sugar. We walked by real Indian tepees and small tents for the soldiers.

"There's the water wagon," said Clara. "Look, the horse tent's clear over there. That's a long way to carry water.

Crowds of people got off the Crocker Avenue Trolley Cars. Scores more came across the Crocker Bridge after exiting the Gratiot Avenue Trolley. Detroit sent extra cars to Mount Clemens for the event. People poured in from all the downtown hotels. The mass of bodies was overwhelming.

We peeked into the horse tent, where cowboys and Cossacks were grooming the animals. We watched Indians having target practice with bow and arrows. We wandered around awe-struck until it was almost seven o'clock.

"Girls, we'd better go to our seats," said Ma.

Pa must have had the same idea. No sooner were we seated than he and the boys showed up.

The tent was different from last summer's circus. A canvas half-tent covered the seats that rose on one side of the arena. On the other side was a canvas fence held up by tall posts. Posters of buffalo, horses, Indians and all sorts of cowboy acts were painted on the canvas. Modern gas-filled globes lighted the field as bright as day.

Soon after we were all seated we could hear music playing. From an opening at the far side the band led a parade of performers, followed by Pawnee Bill and May Lillie.

"Ladeez and Gentlemen," the announcer shouted. "Here he is, buffalo hunter, plains scout, white chief of the Pawnees and Wild West Show-man, Major Gordon Lillie, better known as Pawnee Bill. With him rides his beautiful wife, May Lillie, sharpshooter extrordinaire, champion girl shot of the west!" They waved to the audience.

"And here comes Mexican Joe, Pawnee Bill's right hand man, with his Spanish vaqueros. Joe can rope anything from a wild horse to a rooster."

"Now clap your hands for Indian princess Wynona, equestrian and sharpshooter.

The band continued to play, as cowboys and girls, Indians, and Russian Cossacks all shot pistols into the air and paraded along with all the dazzling acts in full regalia. The whole troop, with ponies and carts, donkeys, steers, and two buffalo made a circle and disappeared again behind the stands. Then the show really got started, with action taking place up and down the field.

"Ladeez and Gentlemen," the announcer began again. "For the first time in the East you have a chance to see a reenactment of a genuine Sioux Cremation Ceremony. Watch chiefs Iron Shell and Good Voice say farewell to their friend Good Deer."

Four Indians with single feathers in their headbands carried a wrapped figure on a wooden platform to the middle of the show ground. Four drummers in loincloths followed them beating out a rhythm. Then came a whole group of Indians; chiefs with buckskin jackets and full war bonnets, and women with colorful skirts. A lone Indian raced across the field with a glowing torch, and set the wrapped figure on fire. As the drums pounded, the chiefs and men danced slowly around the funeral pyre. The women stood behind the dancing men, and wailed loudly, in tones that were not quite a song. As the fiery-blanketed figure burned to ashes, the men carried the platform out of sight, followed by drummers, dancers, women, and chiefs.

When the last Indian disappeared, the announcer began again. "Now, Let's welcome unrivaled equestrian, Lulu Barr, as she masters not one, but two spirited horses!"

Lulu entered the ring at a gallop, standing with one leg on each white horse. Her balance was perfect. She leapt gracefully from one horse to the other. At one end of the field cowboys set a stake on fire.

"You know horses are afraid of fire," said the announcer. "Watch this!"

"I can't believe it!" cried Pa.

Lulu guided the steeds close to the fire and then amazingly, she galloped over the flame with one horse on each side. The crowd cheered. Drums rolled.

Then a stagecoach pulled by six horses came down the field. A group of outlaws raced behind them. With guns blazing they stopped the coach and forced the passengers to disembark. Then Pawnee Bill and his men rode to the rescue, shooting the renegades and sending the coach on its way.

"Did you see that shot?" asked Dan. "Hurrah for Pawnee Bill," he shouted.

At last came the part I was waiting for.

"Now here she is, the star of our show, May Lillie, with her horse, George," called the announcer.

"Look," I said to Clara. "She's riding sidesaddle."

May galloped full-speed around the arena. Ahead of her an aide threw glass balls into the air. Dropping the reins on George's neck, she shot each ball to pieces. Her gun misfired once and George took her back to the gun stand to get another rifle. Off she rode again never missing a shot. At the end of the act George reared up, and May waved as they rode off. May got one of those standing ovations like DeWolfe Hopper got for "Casey at the Bat."

"Ma," I said. "She told me about that horse. She never uses a whip or spurs on him. He always obeys her voice, and if he's not tied up, he follows her everywhere."

"That act calls for perfect coordination between May, the horse, and her assistant," said Pa. "No wonder she is so famous!"

"Here is Mexican Joe," called the announcer. "This man can rope anything from a chicken to an elephant."

Joe twirled his lariat from horseback and then jumped to the ground. He threw his rope in larger and larger circles. He jumped in and out of the whirling circles, and then twirled two ropes at once.

"Watch this," the announcer yelled again. As a horse trotted by the announcer shouted, "Front right." Joe roped the animal on his front right hoof. Then he used his rope on the back hoofs. He roped three horses at a time. At the end of each roping he let the rope slide to the ground so he wouldn't injure the animals.

Then two Indians carried a large board into the center. May Lillie and Princess Wyona took turns standing on it and shooting. At first they aimed at plates an assistant held in the air. Then things got really exciting.

"I can't believe it," said Ma. "Did you see May shoot the ashes off that cigar?"

John jumped up and down. "Look," he shouted. "They're lying down to shoot." They sighted over their shoulders, under their legs, and through a mirror.

"The winner, May Lillie, still our champion rifle shot!" shouted the announcer.

"That's amazing," said Pa. "But it's not as great as what she did on horseback."

There were so many acts I can't even remember them all.

"As a perfect ending," the announcer cried. "We bring you our finest equestrian feat. Here are

Pawnee Bill, May Lillie, and our entire cast dancing the Mexican Contra on horseback."

The stars led pairs of riders circling around the
oval track to a lively Mexican tune. The pairs took
up positions all around the field, and then took
turns crossing the center. In the center they circled
by fours. Next time around they circled in eights.
They changed partners as they went. By the end
they were riding through each other from corner to
corner. If it weren't for the Mexican music, I could
picture a caller shouting, "do-si-do." It was like a
square dance on horseback.

At the end the pairs of horses retreated and
Pawnee Bill and May Lillie rode into the center
waved again. The announcer called, "Goodnight
all!" and the band played, "Goodnight, Ladies."

I clapped until my hands were sore, and John
whistled until Ma made him stop.

Getting through the crowd back to Gratiot took
a long time. There was no question of getting a
crowded trolley home.

"I liked the races best," said John. "They were
really thrilling! The most exciting was the Race of
Nations when an Indian, a Cowboy, a Mexican, and
a Cossack competed."

"No," said Dan. "It was the one where four
racers lay on buffalo hides and held on to a rope
tied to the horses saddle. The poor fellows had to go

three laps around the field and not fall off the hide. Two of them fell off before the finish."

"How about the football game on horseback?" said Elizabeth. "That huge leather ball going up and down the field was hilarious."

"Well, how about the women riders?" I said. "They were every bit as good as the men. Lulu Barr climbed all over that galloping horse. She rode forward and backward, under its belly, and hanging by one leg. It was astonishing! Don't ever tell me that girls can't do anything boys can do!"

"You ought to have gone to the side show," said John. "We saw a Hindu Fakir hypnotize a cobra. It came out of a huge jug and was swaying back and forth to the music from his pipe."

"There was one disappointment," said Elizabeth. "I expected a whole herd of buffalo. Those two scrawny creatures didn't live up to the posters."

The moon was out. John and Elizabeth ran ahead, and my folks were lagging behind. All of a sudden Dan grabbed my hand, and we walked slowly the final blocks home.

It was a perfect end to a perfect evening.

CHAPTER SIXTEEN

REST OF THE SUMMER

The next day, the newspaper had just a couple of comments on the show. Clara found this on the front page and read it aloud: "Pawnee Bill had good crowds yesterday and gave a good show. There was no thievery of any account."

She went on, "It says here that the sheriff raided the train before it left this morning and got a lot of horse blankets and lap robes stolen from farmer's rigs. There were four fellows who were hired and left with the show."

"I wonder who they were?" said John. "There were some older boys working for tickets. Bill, do you know anyone who went?"

"No" said Bill, "But I'll bet they'll be sorry. It must be a hard life."

"Look at this, under 'local jottings,'" I spoke up. "It says 'The artist who is dragged around on his belly by a galloping horse in Pawnee Bill's show gets two dollars a week. No expense spared!'"

"I don't think I'll be running off to join," said John.

After the show, the summer was dull, dull, dull.

John and I were stuck with garden work. We weeded, hoed, and picked bugs off the radishes, carrots, green beans, corn, and tomatoes.

John took over the chickens and egg gathering again in August. I had to help with the canning. Ma, Grandma, and I washed dozens of jars in scalding water and as hot as it was, we had to boil everything in the big canner. We used Grandma's big iron range in the summer kitchen. "Shut the kitchen door," Ma would remind us. "Don't let all this heat into the rest of the house."

The whole house smelled of tomatoes for weeks. "I hate tomatoes," I said. "I hate the smell of them cooking. I hate cutting them in chunks. I hate their squishy looks and their wagon wheel centers.

Ma, you ought to excuse me from the torture of canning them!"

"I'm sorry, Hattie" said Ma. "With Clara working at the hotel, we really need your help."

Grandma'd say, "Let's work on the back porch. I think there's a little breeze."

John decorated his bicycle in red, white, and blue for the August bicycle parade, but he didn't win anything. He complained to Ma, "There were less than a hundred entries. It was better last year!"

In the evenings Elizabeth would call, "Hattie, can you come out?"

"Yes, go Hattie," Ma would say, and I escaped to Elizabeth's, where they had no garden, and life was less hectic. All of our friends gathered there. Sometimes we played Hide and Go Seek. Other times we just sat on the porch and sang. Elizabeth had a set of new stereoscopic pictures of Alaska, and we took turns seeing glaciers and sled dogs and miners panning for gold.

One day John came running home and insisted that we all walk up to the Colonial Hotel. "Grandma, you come, too," he said. "I'll carry Robert."

It was worth the walk. There, parked on the street by the hotel stood an auto-mobile, a horseless carriage. The driver wore a long coat. Goggles covered his eyes. He cranked the engine again and again, and finally it started. He climbed in with two young lady passengers also wearing goggles and long coats. They had on large hats with veils.

Off they drove out of Colonial Court and down Gratiot. I'll bet he got that horseless carriage going a good ten or fifteen miles an hour.

Grandma said, "Mark my words. It'll never be more than a rich man's toy!"

I wonder.

With all the summer work I couldn't quite believe it, but I was looking forward to getting back to school. We went to Prieh's Department Store, and Ma bought some material and some McCall's patterns. Grandma made me three new dresses. I hemmed the skirts myself. Ma let me make them almost as long as Clara's.

Then came the shock that ruined a late August evening.

Dan came running up to where a group of us were sitting on Elizabeth's front porch. "Hey," he shouted. "You won't believe what my ma found in the newspaper!"

He brought out the Macomb Weekly and read, "Miss Ruth Myers will be teaching sixth grade at Grant School this year. Miss Muriel Holt will move on the seventh grade class."

"Not that witch again?" said Elizabeth.

"I couldn't believe what I was reading," said Dan. "How can they do this to us?"

"Oh, no!" I cried. "I wonder if I can bear it." It looks as if the rest of this year of new beginnings will be as unsettling as first eight months. But after all that went on this summer, Miss Holt didn't seem to be as big a difficulty as she had been in January.

"We'll survive!" I told my friends.

NOTES

Pawnee Bill's Wild West Show featuring May Lillie did come to Mount Clemens in the summer of 1900. The show's daybook for July 26 mentions that they had a good crowd.

Grant School was torn down many years ago, and now in 2008 a synagogue has taken its place on South Avenue.

The Colonial Hotel burned to the ground after being empty for many years. Several stores are on the site at Gratiot and Colonial Court.

The house on Smith Street still exists.

In 1900, a Hoffmier family did live in the house, but Hattie and the Hoffmier family in the book are imaginary.

Printed in the United States
218586BV00009B/1/P